Blue's Clues

Hide-and Seek with Blue

by Angela C. Santomero • illustrated by Traci Paige Johnson and Tammie Speer-Lyon

o my Spice Girls! Morgan and Perry—A. C. S.

hanks to Christian Hali & Ian Chernichaw
or their art contributions and for making
ny life sane—T. P. J.

Simon Spotlight/Nick Jr.

SIMON SPOTLIGHT, An imprint of Simon & Schuster Children's Publishing Division, 1230 Avenue of the Americas, New York, New York 10020. Copyright © 1999
Viacom International Inc. All rights reserved. NICKELODEON, NICK JR., Blue's Clues, and all related titles, logos, and characters are trademarks of Viacom
International Inc. All rights reserved including the right of reproduction in whole or in part in any form. SIMON SPOTLIGHT and colophon are
registered trademarks of Simon & Schuster. Manufactured in China   First Edition   10 9 8 7 6 5 4 3 2 1   ISBN 0-689-82445-9

Okay, here we go! Do you see Blue anywhere in here?

Okay, seekers, how are you doing? Are you ready to find Shovel, Pail, and Blue hiding in the backyard? Let's see if we can find them!

Looks like Blue is hiding with Mr. Salt, Mrs. Pepper, and Paprika now! Can you find all of them?

Now find me! Am I hiding in the mudroom?